Ah, it is you. Welcome! As you can see, everyone is here for our big event, and now that we have a Read-ER, this gaze will be even better. You know me, GoTo, from our last adventure. Come on over, don't be shy. I believe you've met everyone, Pen and Carl. SpellGet just couldn't resist letting Carl stay with us, but I have to say it's always great to have a *Woofin* around. He loves this gazing thing too. He sings to the stars and our moons.

Of course, you know Pen-Cil, Felon, Newton, Isaac, Sir Veyor, Catchem, Watchem, and Sir Write-a-Lot.

Hi, Read-ER. Nice to see you again!

Over there, by the wish spinner, are Moester and Milo. They are securing everything so our wishes from tonight's gaze can get through. It probably looks like a large Ferris wheel to you, same idea, really. We even have Stumpers from all around our world joining us, so you see, this is quite an event.

Also, if you look up, that's the TooWoos, Sir Dawg, and the hoo-unds, taking their victory flights. It was a great competition, and it was remarkable to watch, but really, everyone is a winner. I was reading from some of the books in Madam's library about the events you hoo-mans have in your world.  This would be like plane shows, only here, our flyers play games.

Oh, there's SpellGet with more petals. It looks like he may need some help. Pen, could you please tell our Read-ER about the wishes and beginnings of our wish chant? You always explain it so much better than I do.

Well, thanks, GoTo, no problem.

Read-ER, would you like to sit down here on the other side of Carl? Carl is like a big pillow, and he loves the attention. He's only seen one other gaze, so it would be an honor with you on his side.

Now, Read-ER, we all have different ways to make our wishes. Some say it out loud, not the wish, of course, but the wish chant. Some will say it to themselves, but the fun part is both the chant and the wish have to be said simultaneously before the falling stars light fades away, so the story goes. It is quite a challenge. I've found that I have to first chant really fast, and then make one simple wish, which might be the key.

Our wish goes like this:

"A wish from me, so I might be given the wish I wish tonight."

I have also read the hoo-mans chant, and it is very similar to ours.

"I wish I may, I wish I might have this wish I wish tonight?"

Either way, we can all have great wishes! It's fun to see how many falling stars we can spot. The fading of the star happens quite fast, but it is an amazing light show. You just have to smile at the sky and take it all in.

SpellGet, I see you've brought a lot more petals for our friends. Everyone will be so comfortable. I was just explaining the wish chant to our Read-ER.

Excellent, Pen! Well, Read-ER, we should tell you a little more about our skies too. Maybe it will give you a better idea of what we are gazing at. Newton over there is a brilliant sky tracker. He has been studying our skies and stars ever since I can remember. Newton, would you like to come closer and explain more about the wild skies we are going to see tonight?

Sure, no problem. Well, hello again, so nice Read-ER. I'll try not to get too scientific. Understanding some of the trails of the skies involve using big words. I even have problems saying them. I do understand them, but just to make a long story short, the study of different worlds that are just above us is fascinating. SpellGet calls it the wild skies, and I do have to agree. This time of the year the new and old stars come together, so the falling stars do have their fall to gather and give.

What we are about to see tonight comes around once every thirteen quarters and fills the sky, like fireworks in your hoo-man world. We have other falling stars, but they are seen only by chance. They are random sightings and are usually seen in one area at a time. It's like they are practicing their fall. I hope this makes it a little clearer. So, Read-ER, you really did come at the right time. I know I'm rambling on here, but I do hope you enjoy the show!

SpellGet, Read-ER, I can't thank you enough for your help. Okay, which way do we go now, right or left?

Left here I'm sure our Madam-a-la-Muse is already aware of what's happened. Some of her branches just love to watch the gaze from above our field of Daze-zzys. Madam's branches rise so high I often wonder if you're able to see her in your world too.

Ah, SpellGet, you are a wise one and a master of magic, so I have heard. We do see all the wiser trees from all over in our spheres, and they are kind enough to share their great knowledge with us too. Isn't Madam-a-la-Muse a singer also? That's another thing I've heard.

Oh yes, Madam-a-la-Muse has a beautiful voice and so many other talents. Her knowledge is beyond belief. Pen takes great care of her. She's our brilliant librarian. That is where Pen and I met. How did you know I was into magic?

That's easy. You have a glowing Woofin! Only masters can receive that honor, and that is something we do have knowledge of in our books at the academy.

Well, thank you. So that's why Carl glows every time he comes near me, how interesting. I'll have to read more on that subject. And you, DoC Wishful, have you always been a DoC-tar?

Oh yes, all of us in the Wishful family are. We all believe it is our destiny. I also enrolled in the star trailers after my training was done. That's why I was with Page on her fall. My training also taught me a way to breathe in all our galaxies. Really, what's not to love with my job? We heal the sick, help when needed, and get to hear everyone's wonders, dreams, and wishes, even the ancients. That's pretty much my story, and you, SpellGet, are a master of magic in this large land. What an achievement. How did you get started?

I'm not sure about the master part, but I believe it had a lot to do with the help of our Read-ER. Everyone here in StumpsVille has supported me from the beginning, Mama Stump as far back as I can remember. She even had me dreaming about magic before I made my first spell. In my heart, though, I am an adventurer, and I love a great search. And what is a 'Past Key' anyway?

Well, SpellGet, the 'Past Key' is very important. It steers stars while in flight and holds their memories. I will be able to explain more once we get there. I'm not sure what you mean, DoC, but okay. She's not too far now, just around this next corner, just in time. I knew she must have heard something. Her doors are opened. Welcome, DoC-tar, this is our Madam-a-la-Muse.

Oh my, SpellGet, she is a beauty!

Look at that, DoC, there's Pen and the others. She wasn't kidding when she said they would be right behind us. Please go inside. I am sure Pen will be able to help you find whatever you need.

I will have to give Carl a bite of *Bee-Zee* magic before he can fit through the door. Woofin's, as you can see, are very large creatures. The rest of us will wait for Carl.

Yes, DoC Wishful, we found the picture you told us about. Everyone, this is the 'Past Key.' This is what we'll be searching for. There are more notes here too, just a minute. It reads,

In case of a lost or missing 'Past Key,' there are two things that must be done.

One, you must see a glimmer, which is a faint light of color, like a beacon that is color coded to the key before it has been engraved. You must find the color chosen by its owner. It will be written in the *Bright Codes* book.

Two, you must see a glimpse, which is a brief view of where it has been lost, but if it is missing and not lost, there is more. There will be two riddles, handed down by the Riddlers, which will be placed in this book that only one will see. If no one can read beyond what needs to be done, then there will be no team.

And

A rule not to be broken

If you can read beyond this page, know that no one in the Starcademy shall ever be allowed to read the page or be given a chance to see the riddles. They may help but only after someone who is to be part of a team reads the riddle aloud.

We figured out the glimmer part, which would be a color that Page has picked. That should be in the *Bright Codes* book, right, DoC?

Yes, Catchem, colors of the keys, even their codes, among other things, are noted. Watchem, you have a question too? Well, DoC, we understand the beginning, but the riddles from the Riddlers, who or what are they?

Well, Catchem, Watchem, the Riddlers can track a star falling from the star line, but after that, well . . . The Riddlers are the only stars that can hear a signal from a missing or lost key. They can give us clues on how to find it, but they can only write in riddles.

Okay, I need to ask. "There is only one that will be able to read past what is printed on this page" and then under "rule never to be broken," what does that mean?

Only one of you will be able to read past what is on the page, but only if you are the team for the search. The rules were put in place because anyone from the academy would need a team that would be worthy of the search for a missing or lost key. So let's see, Catchem, Watchem, can either of you see anything else past what you have just read'?

Let's see . . . no, there is nothing here, just what we read. And the next page is blank.

So let's pass the book around and see if anyone else can. GoTo, Newton, you try. Can you see anything?

Okay, hmm . . . no, DoC, all we can see is the title and the ways to find it, just like Catchem and Watchem. Here, Pen, Read-ER you try.

Okay . . . No, it's just like the others, nothing. It's blank, like the rest of the pages. SpellGet, Carl, it's your turn. We just need one to continue.

Well, let's see here . . . Yeah, its right here. Look, Carl. Oh, you can't see it either. Hmm . . . really, everyone, it's right here.

Excellent, one problem solved, but now we must pass the riddles that are given. They may give us more information. Please, SpellGet, if you could read it for us?

Sure, no problem. It's saying that we must read the note at the end. If your team and you, I am guessing, can pass the first test, we will be able to move on. Hmm . . . okay, it reads,

Good morn', Mr. More, I'm DoC-tar Think Wishful, and these fine Stumpers are my team. Sorry if I sound like I'm in a hurry, but we are here hoping you would have some information that could help us. It's in regard a missing 'Past Key.' It's not just any 'Past Key,' it's Page Turner's key.

Oh . . . Page Turner's 'Past Key.' Please, all of you come in. DoC-tar Wishful it's nice to see you again. This may turn into quite a search for all of you. The *Bright Codes* book is right here, you'll need her color code first because, as you were saying, it is missing. You must have the riddles from the Riddlers, or you wouldn't be here. I was just about to write down the locations of Bee-A-Fraid and his gang, so maybe I can help you with that too. So this is your team. Please introduce them. I also see you have a glowing Woofin on my steps. What's that beauty's name?

CHAPTER SEVEN

MR. MORE WITH MORE

You would like introductions. Well, Mr. More, on your front steps is our glowing Woofin, Carl, and this is his master, SpellGet. These here are Go-To and Newton. They take care of our maps and course directions. Next, we have Catchem and Watchem. They are our observation and sight-on-scene team. Finally, this is Pen and our Read-ER for our fine points of direction. We were lifted here to your door with the help of Madam-a-la-Muse and her friends.

Well, hello everyone, Madam-a-la-Muse is a dear friend of mine I do hope she is doing well. I've heard she has a bright librarian taking care of her now. I knew you must have a Read-ER with you, or you wouldn't be here knocking on my door asking what you're asking. Read-ER, it is nice to see there is still someone brilliant enough to leap in and take the read the way it should be. Well done. I do hope you are ready for what may come next.

Mr. More, sir. Hi, I am Pen. I am Madam-Muse's librarian, and yes, she is doing very well and has helped us a great deal. Our Read-ER here is like no other. I believe we are ready.

Well, Pen, Page is going to need a good team to search for her missing key. You all look worthy of the task. Okay, here's what I've found for her color. She has written a brilliant blue, and wait, she added sparkles. Hmm . . . interesting stars these days, always wanting just a little bit more. Now remember, a glimpse or a glimmer. Okay, DoC Wishful, that's one thing done. Now do you have your maps with you so I can show you where Bee-A-Fraid and his gang of *Meteorocks* have been reported lately?

Thanks, Mr. More, and yes, the maps are here with Go-To and Newton.

Good, let's lay them out on this table here. Let me see what I have written last. Okay, they were seen here in the Story and in Worthy's, here and here. They have been spreading out to some of our smaller spheres in this area too, but it looks like most of them are sticking around those two galaxies. I hope that helps. Oh yes, Mr. More, it will. Is there anything else we might need to know about them, I mean, the *Meteorocks*?

That seems very true thank you, Ms. When. Now, Ms. Why was there anything out of the ordinary?

Well, DoC-tar, we, I mean all six of us, seen the stars as they flew off to the next galaxy, the Worthy galaxy. We all know she couldn't have made it without all her keys. But because she was crossing the lines, she may have encountered a *Meteorock*. The lines and spheres have been filled with them lately. I'm not sure why.

Okay, Ms. Where, do you think something else may have brought the *Meteorocks* so close?

No. Well, DoC-tar, I do know that What and Page Turner were very close friends and have been forever. She, I mean What, may have seen something we may have missed. I know she was in a hurry to get back to sphere to say a final good luck. If you have a map, I can show you the quickest way to get to What's sphere. DoC-tar, where is SpellGet going?

Please excuse me. I'll be right back. I'm guessing he is going to get our maps.

SpellGet, where are you going *Today*?

I was going to get our maps. If Ms. Where knows the quickest way to Ms. What's sphere, then I believe we may be getting close, DoC-tar. *Today*.

Oh, DoC-tar, this sphere is really getting to me, this language or something. I'm happy for them at least they know what they are saying or to who. Wow, what a new experience!

Okay, I know what you mean. I'll wait here for you, and bring Pen and our Read-ER back with you. They have a better sense of direction on those maps.

CHAPTER NINE

WHAT DOES WHAT KNOW?

shrooms on the trail. We want to place them, just on the outside edge about three steps apart.

This is the last one, DoC-tar. How do we know this will actually work?

Believe me, SpellGet. There will be more than one that will all have to take a stab at them. Okay, let's get back to Carl. We will have to go diving to get through that crack, which will take us to the Sea of Seeing. Carl, we're all here time to go.

Okay, everyone, down. We need to go diving, and it's just a little swimming. Are we ready? SpellGet, is there something wrong?

No, DoC-tar, but I believe I should take Pen's hand to get in. All of you, don't worry, we will be right behind you. Come on, Pen. Hold your breath, and I'll guide us down.

Sounds good, Spells now, everyone this should be a quick swim. Just go toward the glimmer that will be the opening so we'll see all of you on the sands of the Sea of Seeing. Ready set go.

CHAPTER ELEVEN

IT'S ALL WORTH IT

Watch out, everyone. Carl's right behind us. He has a lot of fur and will have to shake off water as soon as he lands. Come over here, Carl. We'll dry you off. Hmm . . . that's odd. He's already dry. What did that?

No worries, SpellGet, this is the Sea of Seeing. And if you fall in wet, you will be automatically dry. I know, I've been here before.

Great idea, we need to get one of these at home for you, Carl.

Everyone, look over there! That has to be the 'Past Key,' and yes it is engraved with Page's name. We did it! Now we have to find Mrs. Sea and see if she knows another trail back to the Starcademy sphere. Hopefully, she will have a trail that is safer than the last one we were on. GoTo, where are you off to?

Well, look, DoC, isn't that one of us? I mean, isn't that a Stumper there by the shore, or did I just walk into a dream? I wonder how she got here. I'm just going to go over and say hi, or is that a bad idea?

No, it's not a bad idea actually it may be a good one. I know her. She was washed ashore here many

quarters ago. No one has come to claim her, so she spends her days here by the shore. Mrs. Sea has always kept an eye on her hoping that someday someone would come. Lately, Mrs. Sea believes she feels very alone in this different world. GoTo, go introduce yourself. We'll stand over here. She will know where Mrs. Sea is. Start by asking her name, just a thought.

Okay, I'm off. Hello there, I'm GoTo. I was thinking we could talk for a bit. Hope I am not being too forward, but what is your name?

No, you are not forward at all. My name is A-Star. Where did all of you come from? I haven't seen any of your kind on our shores here before. You all look

STUMPERS

IN SEARCH
OF THE PAST KEY

BEV SCHOLZ

Order this book online at www.trafford.com
or email orders@trafford.com

Most Trafford titles are also available at major online book retailers.

Print information available on the last page.

ISBN: 978-1-4907-7997-3 (sc)
ISBN: 978-1-4907-7999-7 (hc)
ISBN: 978-1-4907-7998-0 (e)

Library of Congress Control Number: 2016921324

Trafford rev.   05/08/2017

Trafford
PUBLISHING® www.trafford.com
North America & international
toll-free: 1 888 232 4444 (USA & Canada)
fax: 812 355 4082

To my stars,

Fred, Java Jack, Milo, Moester, Molly, and Sadie.

Contents

INTRODUCTION

Read-ER, is that you? Great! You're back! Well, this is excellent! You must have come for a gaze of our *gaze daze*, great timing on your part. This will be our grandest one this quarter.

Please take a short walk with me, so I can explain a little more. You must be wondering what is gaze daze. Well, we are on the trail that leads to *Where Time Slips Away*. That's where the field of *Daze-zzys* grow. I know we didn't get a chance to visit this magical place the last time you were here, but we were so busy searching for our *piece of time* '. Now that all our time is back, there is so much to enjoy. Thank you for that again. We couldn't have done it without you, Read-ER, and now that you know some of our secrets, maybe you can share a few of yours?

Okay, like I said last time, this is a land of make-believe, so when you continue reading, you'll become our size and be able to see our spectacular sight. So I am thinking that you may want to know more about our gaze daze.

Well, this is a festival for all the falling stars that we see tonight. Stumpers from near and far come to this field to watch. They all prepare well in advance. It is a day filled with so many things to do. We have a grand parade, a lot of great food, and lots of treats, games of chance, and races to the wishing well.

We even have a competition for our flying *hoo-unds*. They are our wonderful flying *Dawgs*. When that wraps up we all meet in our field of Daze-zzys to watch the show and maybe even make a wish or two.

I was told that you, *hoo-mans*, also make wishes on falling stars, and now that you will see our show of stars, you might like to make a few wishes of your own. It's not a must, but it is all in fun.

Well, that is the short version of our great gaze. Everyone is going to be so happy to see you again. We are all sitting just around this corner. Please have a seat with the others. I'll be back. I have to get a few more petals from the Daze-zzys. They are kind enough to hand them out for our big event. We use them like big fluffy pillows to look way up into the skies.

Everyone, look who's back—our Read-ER!

CHAPTER ONE

A TIME TO GAZE

Well, SpellGet, it looks like everyone is ready for this one, with all these comfortable Daze-zzy pillows.

Thank you, Newton, and you weren't rambling, and they are definitely wild, but what a pleasure it is to take in the sky's masterpiece. Oh, I think it's about to start. I just saw a little one falling. Lay back everyone, and prepare your wishes!

CHAPTER TWO

A LITTLE MORE THAN GAZING

It's starting. Look, everyone!

Whoa, ah, wow! Isn't that beautiful? And that and that . . . Look over there!

Wow! Spells, do you see that? I've already made two wishes on that star, and I don't want to take me eyes off it, but it doesn't seem to be fading out at all.

Pen, you're right, I think we are looking at the same star, and I believe there may be a problem. It's getting brighter. That can only mean one thing. It's heading straight for us. Everyone, take cover, there's a star coming in fast!

Pen, are you all right? Grab my hand if you can see it through all this glittering dust. Wow, did that star fall fast? Pen, Read-ER, Carl, is everyone okay? I can hardly see any of you.

Yes, Spells, we're all good. Carl and GoTo are on their way to see where it landed. They think it may have hit the wish spinner. SpellGet, this is a first time we've ever been hit by a falling star. Well, it is clearing a bit I can almost see you. Wait a minute. Look over there. Have we seen him around here before, and why is he moving so fast?

No, he must be new. Pen, do you think there may be more to this?

Spells, I am wondering, why there is glitter dust flying off him? Hmm . . . he's carrying a bag with the initials "DTW." He's definitely not from here. Let's join the others and see what's happening.

You're right, Pen. Whoa! Just wait. What's he saying?

Okay, everyone! Please stand back. I am a *DoC-tar*. I see we have a fallen star in need of assistance.

Excuse me, sir. Where did you come from? I didn't see you here before the gaze started. My name is SpellGet, and yours is?

I am DoC-tar Think, DoC-tar Think Wishful. I was right behind the falling star trailing in the stardust.

She is a star in training, but I must see what happened to her. There has never been a star fall into Where Time Slips Away before. That is where we are, right?

Yes, this is Where Time Slips Away. Is there something we can do? She doesn't look very well. Is there more that can happen?

No, no, we cannot guess just because we think there may be a problem. But it may just be that, a problem. This is very rare. We should step away from this glitter dust and let her rest. Then we may see what we can do. SpellGet, may I have a brief word with you? Let's walk.

Of course! But, DoC Wishful, I must insist that our Read-ER come with us.

You have a Read-ER! Oh my, I am sorry. I didn't know! A Read-ER here now, well this is an honor. Hello! Yes, yes, please walk with us.

SpellGet, would you have a *Wiser Tree* nearby? I would like to do some research, and I may need some help. I believe there may be more to her fall than I can explain. It would be easier to show you.

Yes, Doc-tar we do have a *Wiser Tree*. Her name is Madam-a-la-Muse. Just a question, though, could what happened be because of someone's wish?

Oh no, that could not happen, SpellGet, not to my knowledge. It's not even on the wish scale. We will need to see her, your wiser tree, I mean. The star that has fallen is Page Turner. She's Book Turner's second daughter. And this morning she had an assignment to hand out *random acts of kindness*, just a few at a time so that she may gain the wisdom of patience. It is in one of the steps to begin in the more difficult programs of the *Starcademy*. Are you familiar with our world?

I know a little, DoC-tar but only from the books that I have read in our Madam's library. We are aware of the *Starcademy*, and Mr. Book Turner, isn't he the creator of our realms?

11

Yes, SpellGet, he is the creator and the full *Presence* of our galaxies. This little one, Mrs. Page, here is very new to the falling apart. This was only her fifth jump from the Starcademy and her third jump from the Star Line. I'm just not sure until I examine her again, if it was her steering off course or maybe something else that would make her fall so far off her mark. It just doesn't make sense, but I think there may be more to this than we know.

Please continue, DoC-tar.

Just a minute, you two I see all the stardust has fallen. I will check to see if she's all right. I have to check her points, and I do hope she hasn't lost her keys. Excuse me; I'll explain more when I get back.

Keys. How interesting, hmm . . .

SpellGet, Read-ER! Who was that? I mean the fluttering stardust guy who just ran past me, or was that the DTW guy?

Actually, one and the same, Pen. The glitter guy and the DTW, his name is DoC-tar Think Wishful. He was just explaining how the star may have landed here. So what do you think? Is the star awake yet? Has she said anything?

Yes, but not really awake. It is more like she's in a dream. She has been going on about losing something, the past, random acts books, a cover, and even going on about a Woofin. I'm thinking that was when Carl was standing over her, her eyes briefly flashed open. Then she went on saying something about keys, and well, the list was long. GoTo really helped in settling her down, but hopefully, the DoC-tar can tell us more.

That's interesting. The DoC-tar also said something about keys just before he left us to check on her. We did find out the star's name though. It's Page Turner. Pen, remember that book about the Starcademy? Well, Page is one of the founder's daughters. I think DoC-tar Wishful might need our help. What do you think?

Really, that's the daughter of the big guy? Wow, the *Presence* of stars! Oh, you know we have to help SpellGet!

There he is. Let's see what we can do for him. DoC-tar Think Wishful, sir, this is my friend Pen. We were just talking, and if you need anything, please feel free to ask.

Thanks so much, Pen, for tending to her so quickly. You and your friends would be a great help to me, but I must warn you, it may be quite a challenge.

When I was checking Page, GoTo introduced himself, and the big glowing furry one said his name was Carl. He is a Woofin, yes and who does he belong to, SpellGet?

Well, Carl, I would like to say he's mine, but we all love him so much he's just became part of the family. He brought us home from a lengthy journey and then asked if he could stay, and who could say no to that?

SpellGet, well done! A Woofin in your Ville, they are so devoted, loyal and he is glowing. You know what that means, right?

Not really. I have read a little on the famous glow, something about a master of magic and some Woofin stuff, but not enough to know exactly what it means. So DoC, about Page, what's her condition will she be all right? And about the keys, what does that all mean?

SpellGet, I will let you know about the key. Page will be fine for now and will hopefully not wake up until we find her 'Past Key.' That's what's missing.

I have given her some wishful dreams and the air she needs to stay comfortable, calm, and without any worries. Pen, would you be as kind as to find someone to stay with her for a while?

Yes, DoC Wishful, not to worry. Is there anything else we can do? We do have a great team of searchers, and it sounds like that may be just what you need.

I'm so glad you asked, Pen. That's a yes with a very big please. A team of searchers are just what we'll need, but be careful when asking because they will be traveling up, very far up. It will be quite a journey searching for a 'Past Key.' I can explain more once we reach your Madam-a-la-Muse.

Well, Spells, Read-ER, the DoC needs our help, so please show him the way to our Madam-a-la-Muse. I will find someone for Page and pick out our team for the search. We'll be right behind you.

Thank you so much, Pen. Oh yes, one more thing. Please bring your Woofin, Carl I know we'll need him too.

Not a problem. Carl loves the P word, but his favorite is a great S! That means play or search—the search is on!

Chapter Three

Going To learn more

Okay. Hi again, Pen. I must say your Madam-a-la-Muse is magnificent. Look at these stairs and her cases. Such beauty and knowledge all in one place Wiser trees are so impressive. Hello! In here, Madam! Pen and I, DoC-tar Wishful, are here, in need of your wisdom and knowledge.

Hello, Pen, and a thank you very much, DoC-tar Wishful! All those compliments at once, I have to catch my breath. I do believe we have just what you've come for. I was told by one of my branches a star has fallen in Where Time Slips Away, but she is not just any fallen star, is she?

No, I am afraid not. She is Book Turner's daughter. I have put her in a state of dreams and added our spheres air to surround her. I've found that her 'Past Key' is missing, and you know that it may become very tragic if we are unable to find it soon.

You're right. We must move quickly. There's no time to waste. Pen, all the information you will need is in the star section to your left on the second tier. If I remember correctly, you may need all five books to find out where to go from here.

Okay, thanks, Madam, DoC Wishful. Please take a seat. The team will be in right away, and I'll be back with the books we need. Oh, there's SpellGet now. I won't be long.

Carl! Carl! I know you want to say hello to DoC Wishful, but watch your tail! Sorry about that, DoC-tar he always goes into this tail—wagging mode when he's fed some *Bee-Zee* magic. He will settle down in a bit. I will introduce you to the rest of our crew.

This here is GoTo, our go-to guy. He is brilliant, and if there's anything you may ever need or have to have, he's the one.

Well, GoTo, we met at Page's landing, or should I say her mishap. And thanks so much for being so helpful. It's great to see you here!

I'm more than happy to help, DoC! I do have to say the stardust that you came in on was beautiful.

Well, thanks so much for noticing, GoTo. I do try, and you three are?

Hello, DoC-tar, I am Catchem. This here is Watchem, my partner in observation, and this is Newton, our specialist of space and time. It is a pleasure to meet you. I do wish it was under different conditions, but we are all here to help, so where do we begin?

I would like to thank you all for being here. Please have a seat. We have to figure out where to start. Great, there's Pen. Let me you help you with those books.

CHAPTER FOUR

MORE OF SOME STORIES

Now I will give you all a brief update about the fallen star. Her name is Page Turner. Her mission was to hand out random acts of kindness. I work closely with the Turner family. Mr. Book Turner requested I follow in Page's stardust as she is a very young star. Now the 'Past Key,' as we call it, is missing. It is one of three keys that are given to the stars. The *Past* is their memories and steering in flight. There is a *Past*, a *Present* and a *Future*. Their keys will be engraved with their names once they have passed all of the tests. With all three engraved, it gives them a chance to find their own destiny. Our search is to find Page's missing 'Past Key without it, she cannot continue.

What do you mean, DoC, she can't continue?

Glad you asked, SpellGet. Continuing is part of a star's schooling. Page losing her 'Past Key' means she may not be able to remember any of her past, and I mean nothing.

Oh . . . that's not good. Where should we start looking, Doc?

Well, SpellGet, we'll start with these books, and maybe we can get a plan together. Catchem, Watchem, I think this one could be a good start. Please look up the 'Past Key' and anything about a missing key.

Hmm, *Key to Keys*, an interesting title. So this book should have a picture of the 'Past Key,' am I right?

Yes, and maybe something else we could use. This one, SpellGet and Carl, look up Woofin's and their masters, I believe what you'll be looking for is in chapter 2.

No problem. *The Key to Travel* is also interesting, don't you think, Carl? Okay, okay, enough with the wagging tail. Let's get into this book.

This one Flying for the Stars GoTo and Newton, you will be looking for locations from the star lines to the Story and Worthy galaxies, and if you could also look for cracks in both areas, thank you.

Okay, this sounds great. Hmm . . . check this out, Newton. It even has pictures all over it. Hey, Doc, what do you mean we have cracks in your galaxy?

Yes, GoTo, we do have cracks, not really in our galaxies but in the spheres that make up the galaxy. You call yours planets, which, in turn, make up your galaxy. Our spheres are constantly shifting as time goes by, which creates cracks on their surface. We say all great things get better with age.

Okay . . . and about the Worthy and Story galaxies, what is that?

Well, GoTo, Newton, the Story galaxy is made of six shining spheres. We call them Who, What, Where, Why, and How. They spread piles of stardust for our stars on the star lines. The dust makes the show you see from here more exciting. Now on to the Worthy galaxy,  it is made of three ancient spheres called Trust, Honesty, and Truth. That is where the Random Acts stream flows and even the cracks there can put you in different realm.

Interesting, okay, let's get to work, Newton. Wow, there's a lot of information in here!

And this last one, *Shining Down*, Pen, Read-ER, is all about the stars being sharp and being able to find the shine of the *key*. If you could, please look up the third and fifth jump from the star line, so we can be sure if Page's 'Past Key' didn't fall here. It may have suggestions about where we can find it.

Just a minute, we only have four, but there should be five. That would be *Bright Codes*. Madam-a-la-Muse, is there one missing, or could it be somewhere else?

You're right, DoC-tar Wishful. Pen gathered what was there, but I see you only have four. Pen, if you could, please check our visitor log and the last entries in our borrowed books.

Yes, absolutely, it's right here, and yes, the borrowing log says that the book, DoC, has been signed out two times recently by a Mr. Learnerd More. I can also see that he is from the Starcademy, and the book hasn't yet returned. DoC Wishful, do you perhaps know a Learnerd More. I know it's a big academy, but maybe you know him?

Learnerd, Learnerd, hmm . . . oh yes, Mr. More. I should have known that's where the book is. He would have to update. I'm not sure why I didn't remember his name.

I must tell you all Mr. More has two very important jobs: One is to add the new stars who graduate to *The Bright Codes* book, and the other is to keep the stars informed of where Bee-a-Fraid and his gang of *Meteorocks* may be at any given time.

We should definitely speak with him first. I'm sure he will be able to give us more information. Yes, Pen, it looks like you have another question?

I do. What are the *Meteorocks* and who is Bee-a-Fraid?

I thought you would ask that. Well, a *Meteorocks* is a star's worst nightmare. They attack in packs. They are swirling pieces of sharp rocks with very bad attitudes. They are able to take over an entire star and can either hurt or destroy them completely. Bee-a-Fraid is their leader. That is why Mr. More is so important all of the stars. That was a short explanation, but we can find out more when we get to the Starcademy. So, Catchem, Watchem, did you find what we need in that first book?

Chapter Five

Just a riddle away

As a team, which one are you?

1. *One to make a bubble that flies with paws*
2. *One that will go to seek a star and add another*
3. *One very fine point that will have to be made*
4. *One mind of stars that shows the truth*
5. *One that sees trouble beyond the time*
6. *One that has caught with ease*
7. *One that glows with a nose that knows*
8. *One that needs to continue a story*

Okay, that's it for the first riddle. I think it's asking us who we believe we are. So let's choose. What do you think, Pen, Read-ER?

Good idea. Let's all take some paper and write down the number we think we are. Then, SpellGet, you can tell us, after we are done, if we got this right or not.

SpellGet, I believe we're done. This is all of us.

Give me a minute. Ahh . . . hmm . . . I'm thinking this is great. We all seem to know who we are here. There're no doubles. Okay, from the top. I am number one, I said was two is GoTo, three is Pen, four is Newton, five is Watchem, six is Catchem, and seven is our Carl, and yes, we have number eight, ah . . . it has to be our Read-ER. I believe that's it, good job everyone, ok DoC, now what?

SpellGet, if we are all right, the second riddle should be showing up on the next page. Can you see anything?

Hmm . . . yes, there's something here. It says, "Things you may need." Okay, I'll read aloud.

The Things You May Need

A brilliant branch to start,

Many blades of green,

Needles from your ever,

Rope Vines from the forest with extra to spare,

Shields from the Wiser,

Puffer shrooms,

Pairs of glove-'n '-paws for all plus one,

Many Berries of green,

And find a Star that is.

So that's all of it. DoC-tar do you have any suggestions, or ideas. Where should we go from here?

Well, it sounds like we may be in for some battles to recover this 'Past Key.' For example, on the first one, it says we will be needing blades of grass. On the second, I'm guessing your larger stumps bare large needles. And on the third, rope vines. All of that combined will make a fine blade.

So the rest, what do you think DoC? Please continue. We all have to know this.

The fourth sounds like leaves for shields. We'll ask Madam-a-la Muse if she could help us with that. The fifth, are your puffer shrooms, if they are grazed or touched in our galaxy, they will give off a mist that will put them to sleep long enough for us to get away. Don't worry none of you will be affected because they are from your world.

The glove-'n '-paws, with some of your magic, SpellGet, would be used to throw the berries. It will help them sail further, and they will explode where you were looking. I'm not sure of the last one, but maybe it might come to us later.

GoTo and Newton, have you come across anything we can use. I'm thinking it may be a line off the Starcademy to the other galaxies. Any luck?

Well, DoC, we believe so. Newton has brought in his tools and is now figuring the distances between a few lines but we did find the cracks in the Story and Worthy galaxies, like you said.

Good work on the two galaxies, one of them is where Page would have picked up her dust, and the other is the stream. Okay now, SpellGet, Carl, what have you found?

Well, DoC-tar, it is making points on how to travel. It says, "When you want to leave the sphere of the Starcademy, you will need an *En-Circle* to reach any other destination between the spheres or a run for the trails."

We are thinking that would be because the air we would be breathing up there is different from ours here. The *En-Circle* looks like a big bubble, but if we run into that Bee-a-Fraid and his gang, wouldn't they be able to burst it?

No, SpellGet, they can give us a lot of trouble for sure, but they wouldn't be able to break through your *En-Circle* because it will be made from your magic.

Oh okay, and then it goes on to say, "Going through any new star line or cross into a new galaxy, you will need a ticket from the *keeper*."

So, DoC, who or what is that?

Ah yes, the *safe keeper*—she monitors all that comes and goes off the star lines. We won't need a ticket because Carl will be glowing when we pass. Woofin's are precious to our spheres. They even have their own galaxy. That's why you two are so important. You and Carl are not only our transportation up but also back. Pen, it's your turn. What have you and our Read-ER found?

There are a few things, DoC-tar Wishful. The book speaks of directions to move around the dangers we may face, but it doesn't really get into much detail. One thing though, could you explain more of what's out there and what we may come across?

Good point, Pen. Okay, the Story and the Worthy galaxies have some interesting things. The planets themselves all have their own spheres, but because they are so close together, there is a lot of opposition. They have very unpredictable weather, rock showers, and ray twisters that come without warning. The Worthy Galaxy has become somewhat of a battlefield after Honesty spoke to Trust without Truth. We may encounter the *Meteorock* gang. All of these will be a threat. Then there is Sea from the Sea of Seeing, which has remained calm for quarters, but lately, I'm not sure. I could go on but I think you understand.

GoTo, you look confused. Do you have a question? Yes . . . hmm . . . let me get this straight. We are to spring up to your so called Starcademy and to jump into a bubble on Carl to connect us to a trail that may scoot us up even further into outer space to the worst possible surroundings that may be beyond our scariest imaginations just wondering?

GoTo, there is no other way to say this, but yes, you are correct.

Okay, hmm . . . another question, DoC how are we getting up to the Starcademy? Because it looks like it's way up there.

Good question, GoTo. Hmm . . . Madam-al-a-Muse, would you have any ideas or suggestions for us? I think we're at a standstill.

DoC-tar Wishful, I'm glad you asked. I believe I do have an idea. You know, my branches reach up far. In fact, it can reach right into your yard, or should I say, the Starcademy backyard with all of you on Carl's back. It shouldn't be too hard. What do you think?

Yes, what a brilliant idea! Great, another problem solved. Okay, let's get started, everyone. Gather the things we need from our list, and let's find this lost 'Past Key'! Thanks so much, Madam-a-la-Muse.

It has been a pleasure to help you all. Oh, and another thing, the best shields will be found at the top of my branches in the backyard of the Starcademy. They are the strongest and will be just what you need. My limbs caretaker Mayday will know.

Thanks again! Okay, let's get this search started, looks like Carl is already out the door.

DoC-tar, I warned you, just say the S word, which, of course, means "search" to him, and he will always be more than ready.

So what does the P mean again?

We try not to say it much because, as you have seen, he is one big Woofin. It means "play ball," but we need one big ball. We have Newton and his friend Isaac creating one now, but it is still a work in progress, so we don't say the word often.

PLAY BALL

OR **SEARCH**

Chapter Six

The Way Up

Doc, I believe we have all the things we need from the Riddle's' list, but we're all a little confused about putting the blades together. Can you give us a hand?

Absolutely! Okay, your blades of grass are like swords in our galaxy. So just take one blade and one of the needles. Now twist the vines around the bottom of the grass like this. We're done.

Thanks, DoC that makes sense. Okay, Carl, are you ready? Let's get this started!

You bet. I'm ready! Spells, did you write down that spell, the one about the bubble thing, the *En-circle*? Oh, and there it is.

Carl, you're the one with the nose that knows. I'm thinking we may need it to cross some of the sky lines that GoTo and Newton found. All right, everybody, climb up. DoC-tar Wishful, please stand behind us, a first journey on a Woofin maybe a little bumpy. Just remember, you have to hold on tight.

Thanks, SpellGet. Madam-a-la-Muse, it was a great pleasure to meet you, and thanks for everything we will see you on the way back.

The pleasure was mine, DoC-tar Wishful. Have a safe trip. I hope you find the key you are searching for soon for Page's sake.

Is there anything else we might need to know, Madam?

Yes, but this need to know is for Carl. Okay, to begin, there will be three caretakers of my branches that will be lifting you. The first one is Maple. She will guide you to the second. Her name is Oak. Then our third there is quite a leap, so be careful. Once you have landed, you will meet Mayday. She will show you to a red door. That is the office of Mr. Learnerd More. Carl, do you have any questions?

No questions, Madam-Muse. Three up and three down, thank you. Oh, look over there. That must be Maple coming our way. She's quick.

Hi! I'm Maple, and just so you all know, I was taught by Madam-a-al-Muse, so don't worry. It will be a fast trip up, so everyone hold on tight. Carl, place your paws here. Don't worry; it won't hurt the *En-Circle.*

Wow, you weren't kidding. Maple, that was fast! Is that Oak over there?

Yes, now remember, Carl, there is a leap from Oak to Mayday, as Madam-Muse was saying. Mayday will take you to Mr. Mores' red door, and have your

shields ready. On your trip back, the three of us will be waiting for you, so be careful up there.

Thanks, Maple, and we will be seeing you soon.

SpellGet, Maple wasn't kidding about the leap to Mayday from Oak. Is everyone okay?

We're all okay. That must be Mayday. I can see she's carrying the shields.

Hi, I'm Mayday. Madam-Muse said your team may need these for your journey and that I am to show you to Mr. Mores' red door. Follow me; it's just around the corner. There it is the famed red door. Good luck and take care!

Okay, everyone, there's no turning back now. Just a simple knock, we will see where this will take us. I don't believe I will have to introduce you all as Mr. More will probably ask you first.

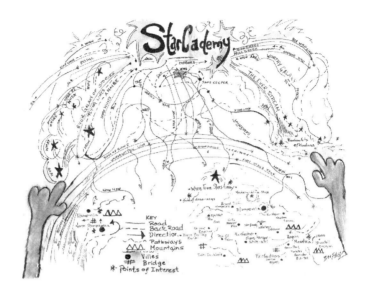

Let me see . . . oh yes, they can only see in black and white. That's why we have color-coded the keys. You must be careful though. If a *Meteorock* finds out a key is missing, they will want to steal it before the owner can recover it, and we don't want to know the rest of that story, as it wouldn't end very well for any of us.

A few more things, SpellGet, getting to the next sphere wouldn't be a problem with your glowing Woofin. I'll be giving you some of this—it is Will-It-Away dust. If you mix it with your Bee-Zee magic, it becomes even more powerful. It is called this because if you need something or someone away from you and your team, you can sprinkle just a pinch to make them go away. Just remember, the spell won't last long, but it will give you enough time to find cover or move on.

Thank you. It is so nice to see you have magic here too! Is there any more we should know?

A few things, stay close to your team. Carl, always fly with grace and land softly. It will make it easier to catch the glimpse or a glimmer from the key. You will be starting in the Story galaxy, which may cause you to be speechless. That is where Page would have gathered her stardust. So stay focused. In the Story galaxy, they may put a spell on you because you are traveling with a Woofin. They love Woofin's, so stay close to your Carl. Another thing, if you find anyone in your team acting unusual, you must say the word *Today*. It will dismiss the spell and let you carry on. Their galaxy has thousands upon thousands of stories; so again, all of you must stay focused. Be careful on the trails between the two galaxies. If necessary, use the tools the Riddlers suggested. There is always a reason to their rhymes. One other thing, if Carl smells smoke, take cover in your *En-Circle*. I believe that's the most I can give you. Take care of each other. Hope to see all of you again. DoC-tar Wishful, is that a deal?

It's a deal, Mr. More. Thank you so much for all your help. SpellGet, it looks like Carl is waiting for his *En-Circle.*

You're right, DoC. Let's get this search going! Ok one, two, and three. There it is. Okay, everyone, let's go. Hold on tight to Carl. It's off to the Story galaxy. Just remember, Carl, your nose knows, so let's find that key.

Woofin in!

Chapter Eight

What Do You Mean, Storynese?

DoC-tar I believe Carl is doing well with our Encircle. What do you think?

Well, SpellGet, you were right. It is a little bumpy, but it's a great ride. Mr. More forgot a few things about the Story galaxy.

What do you mean forgot something? There's more? DoC-tar, you're not letting me feel warm and fuzzy like Carl does. So he forgot what part?

I will tell you when we land, okay? Now, Carl, this is Mrs. Who and Mr. How's sphere, so remember what Mr. More said land softly. Catchem, Watchem, the key might be found on the stardust trails. Please watch for the glimmer. GoTo, Newton, if you could please point them out, and Pen and Read-ER, stay close for a point of direction. If we can't find it here, we will have to keep searching. Remember, stay close to Carl in this galaxy. We don't want him drawn into their stories, and again, stay focused. *Today.*

Okay, everyone, the DoC and I are just going to step away for a moment.

What is it, DoC--tar; you just said that word *today?* Are you confused?

No, but the team looked a little out of the ordinary, so *today* was, I believe, in order. Okay, what Mr.

More forgot was the reason why we need the word here. In this galaxy, they have a slightly different language from ours. They call it storynese. So it might be a bit difficult to understand. I'm thinking we will just have to ask the right questions.

DoC, I don't know storynese! So what is this something out of nowhere? Okay . . . where did this so-called language, storynese, come from? So we need to know something more? What do I think! Well, Mr. DoC-tar Wishful guy, what do I really think? What do I say to the team? You want me to walk back to them and say something like, "Okay, everybody, just don't speak and stand back because our speakenese is too storynese for these guys," or is it the other way around? Whoa, I don't know where that came from. I'm sorry.

No, no . . . SpellGet, *Today.* Stay focused. I'll let you know more. Okay, SpellGet, snap out of it. Now are you with me again?

Yes, that was interesting. I didn't even know what came out of my mouth.

Its okay, SpellGet, it's just the sphere getting to you. I have to thank Mr. More for letting us now the latest word *today* and we may need to keep speaking it to keep each other focused, okay?

Okay, now tell me more about this storynese language thing. Is there more to it?

Well, just a little. It was passed down to the Story spheres from the *Content* of the ancients of the Worthy galaxy. Content is their beginnings, so the less we speak here, the more we might be able to learn. It will be tricky at first, but we need any information they can give us. I was thinking that just the two of us should talk with them and keep the team at a distance. What do you think?

Okay, let's do this *Today*. I think I'm getting what you are saying. I'll let the team know. Be right back.

Everyone, the DoC-tar and I are going to meet Mrs. Who and Mr. How, so please stay here. If you could, Pen, please firmly hold on to Carl. We all need to stay focused and to remember what Mr. More said. *Today* is the word.

Not a problem, SpellGet. We will be right here. If there's anything you need, just let us know.

Stay close Spellget, now it begins. Hello, we would like to speak with Mrs. Who and Mr. How, please.

Yes, they are both in. May I know who's asking?

Yes, of course, I am DoC, DoC-tar Think Wishful from the Starcademy, and this is SpellGet from StumpsVille. We just have a few questions. If I may ask, who are you? I can't remember seeing you here in this galaxy before.

That's interesting. My name is Content. I'm here a lot to showcase their stories. Mind you, my office is in the back, so that might be why haven't seen me. I was just passing the door when I heard your knock. I will let them know you are here, and then it's time for my walk.

SpellGet *Today* Okay, stay focused.

I am *Today* DoC, this is getting tiresome.

DoC-tar Wishful! So nice to see you again please come in. I see you have met Content. She is here taking care of a few beginnings. It is always nice to have her around. Hmm . . . I see you have guests also. May I ask why you are here? Content was saying you have some questions.

Could you wait just one moment, Mr. How.

SpellGet, Content only shows up when there is a problem or . . . a beginning or an end. Could you please follow her and make sure she doesn't get too close to Carl?

Yes, we have a few questions, sir. It is about a missing key. It may have fallen while packing up for this quarter's event of the falling stars. If you may have any information, it may be helpful for our search.

So you are searching for a missing 'Key'? This must be a very important 'Key' for you to come all this way and with a team?

Yes, Mr. How and Mrs. Who, this key is one of a kind. It belongs to Page Turner.

You mean Page Turner—the Page Turner, Mr. Book Turner's daughter?

Yes, and we do hope you can help us or at least give us some idea of where to continue.

Oh my! Maybe the girls have seen her lately. Our stories take pride in seeing who comes and goes and where and what's up. Who, dear, where are the girls, or have they gone home?

I'm not sure, How, but I will check if they are still here. I have noticed there is a glowing Woofin out there. He looks fantastic. We just love them, and we have so many stories!

Yes, Mrs. Who, and that would be SpellGet's glowing Woofin. He is his master from StumpsVille. If you could please, Mrs. Who, find out if the girls are still here.

Of course, DoC-tar, I will be right back. Oh, excuse me, Content that was a fast walk. Oh, watch out, SpellGet is right behind you. Content, have you seen the girls around?

Yes, before I went out, they were in the Sphere room. They should still be there.

So, SpellGet, how did you come to team up with DoC-tar Wishful?

Well, sir, that was easy. He needed help, and we are the best searchers in our land. At least that's what we've heard.

So tell me more. You know that with Content here, there may be more of a beginning, and with Who, What, Where, When, Why, and of course, myself, How. They will be joining us soon, so you might want to share some of your stories with us. Would you be interested?

Mr. How, I am sorry to cut short this chat you are having with SpellGet, but *Today*, we are in such a hurry. We have to get back with the key, some other time maybe?

Okay, DoC-tar Wishful. Mrs. Who should be up soon. Oh there she is. Page Turner must have veered off course, missing her key. So where did she fall?

She landed in Where Time Slips Away, which is StumpsVille territory in the other realm of Genuine.

I believe we've heard of that realm, and hmm . . . StumpsVille, really? That's the one with the brilliant show of stars. They call it Gaze Daze, I believe. Am I right?

Yes, it is a very big event for all the Stumpers.

No matter which key it is, DoC-tar, I do hope we can help. Let me introduce you. These are our stories, When, Where, Why, and we have one missing, Who. Where would What be?

My dear How, you know What. When she has her mind set, it's her way or no way. Sorry, DoC-Tar Wishful and SpellGet. What has been a little off her sphere for a while. I think it's because of the Ever galaxy, which has been moving closer because of the *Meteorocks*.

That's okay, Mrs. Who. We will get right to the questions for the stories you have here. Now, Ms. When, Why, and Where, when did you last see Page Turner on or near your spheres?

Well, DoC-tar, we did see Page on our lines when she was collecting her dust, but that is normal for this time of the quarter, and she didn't seem to be missing anything. Maybe there is more to the story than we think.

Hi, guys. We need the maps, GoTo and Newton. These stories may help us look further, and again, stay close to Carl. I believe that Content is here somewhere, and that's a whole story in itself. I will have to tell you later. Pen, Read-ER, the DoC-tar asked if you could come along for directions. These spheres have strong senses, and just as Mr. More said, remember the *Today*.

Okay, SpellGet, we will try our best *Today*.

Please come in. Why, our quests are back, and you were saying you may be able to help them.

Well, hello again, SpellGet, DoC-tar and you are?

Hi, Ms. Why, I am Pen and this is our Read-ER. We are hoping you can help us.

Well, hello, a Read-ER, so nice to meet you! Oh yes, you need the quickest way to What's sphere. Hmm . . . it's this way. But stay away from the Evers right here, or they may pull you in, which is not good. Okay, after that, take two lefts, then three rights, and you will be right at her door. We hope What can help you more than we have.

No worries, Ms. Why every little thing may be able to help. SpellGet, *Today*. Okay, you three, let's get back to Carl and keep moving. Pen, did that help?

I think so, but Carl's nose might know best. Once I show him the map and with his paw power, we should be there in no time, and Catchem and Watchem will be looking for the glimpse or the glimmer.

Okay, Carl, look here. This is where we are going, past these four spheres to this one. It's Ms. What's sphere, and if we can't see any glimmer or glimpse, we will have to move on to the Worthy galaxy.

Okay, I see what you're saying. Everyone, hold on. This is going to be fast.

Carl, you are brilliant! And that was a quick and a graceful landing. Okay, let's look first. Catchem, Watchem, did you see anything, any glimpse or glimmer?

DoC, I am afraid not. Watchem, anything?

Sorry, Doc, nothing here. GoTo, Newton?

Okay, nothing here, Pen. We should go in and at least introduce ourselves as we are on Ms. What's sphere. Maybe she can help.

Carl, can you find anything with that nose of yours, any smells at all?

Nothing yet, DoC wait, there's something in the air. It smells like smoke, everyone, take cover under me now. I'm still in the En-Circle! It must be the *Meteorocks*. That's what I see, and it looks like they have smaller ones following them. Now what, DoC?

You're right, Carl. They look like mini *Meteorocks*. Everyone, grab a pair of glove-'n'-paws and berries. We may need to distract them. SpellGet, we'll need your magic, so touch as many berries as you can.

All of you will be safe here in the En-Circle. Just keep low. We really don't want these guys on our trail. I have to speak to Ms. What. I'll slip out here and get to her door. Be back as soon as I can.

Who's there? Where did you come from? Why are you here?

Ms. What, I am DoC-tar Wishful from the Starcademy. May I come in? I think you may be able to help us.

With what? And yes, please come in, DoC-tar. I've been worried since the *Meteorocks* have been sneaking around our spheres. What is it, DoC-tar? What do you think I may be able to help you with?

Long story short, Ms. What, Page Turner has lost her 'Past Key' and the Stumpers search party is here, helping. We were told you where very close to Page. Did you see anything out of the ordinary when Page left with her dust, and was she on her way to the Worthy galaxy?

Oh, poor Page. Well, out of the ordinary, hmm . . . There was something. I did notice a glimmer after saying our good-byes, but to get to the Random Acts stream, she would have had her keys. Maybe the *Meteorocks* saw it too, the glimmer, I mean. So if that is the case, that could be why they are hanging around. One thing I did notice with the *Meteorocks*, they have their trainees trailing them. They are the ones to watch out for. If they try and circle you, dive for a trail. It will be safer. Do you have what the Riddlers' notes said?

Yes, thanks. You have been a great help. We have to hurry. Time is running short.

Take care, DoC-tar Wishful and your team. One more thing, please let Page know that I miss her and to be safe.

I definitely will, Ms. What, and thanks again for your help.

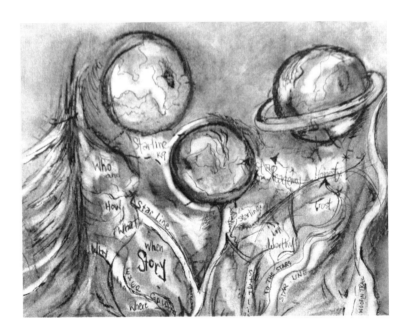

CHAPTER TEN

ON THE WAY TO THE WORTHY'S

I'm back, and I do believe we have more information. We still have all the berries, and it looks like they are just passing over us for now. Well done.

DoC-tar, are we finally finished with the *today* thing?

Yes, SpellGet, I believe. Okay, Ms. What said that the *Meteorocks* may have seen a glimpse too, so we really have to be careful here. Carl, we are going to start off slowly. We do not want to stir up the *Meteorocks*. We need to stay low, so we can get on top of the trails, and then you know it from there?

Yes, I do, DoC GoTo, Newton, and Pen have been going over them again with me. Just let me know when we can speed up, okay?

Okay, good idea. Now, Catchem, Watchem, I believe this could be our greatest chance to see a glimpse or glimmer if it is here. As soon as you do, tell Pen and our Read-ER, they will be able to find the direction, if you could please.

Oh my, Spell-Get, Go-To, Newton, I need you to look at this.

Is that what I think it is, DoC? I'm thinking it's one of the trainees from the gang, right? And it is heading straight at us.

You're right! You four, keep looking for the glimpse. Stay here in the En-Circle. Carl, we need to land quickly on one of the trails. Pick the one closest to us. Pen, direct him, please. We need to get this little one away before he lets the rest of the gang know that we are here.

Okay, DoC, that wasn't a graceful landing, but we're down. The trails let us breathe here, right?

Yes, Carl, but we will need you to stay here. I'm thinking a lot of speed may be necessary to get back to the lines. Everyone, grab the blades and shields. If this doesn't work, we will have to try something else.

Okay, it's time. GoTo, Newton, stand on the opposite side of SpellGet. What we are trying to do here is to not destroy the little one, but to take off the sharp edges on his outside. He's coming fast. I will have to distract him. Everyone, find a point and slice. Okay, DoC, this is working, but I thought you said this is just a little one?

Keep slicing, and yes, this is a little one, probably taken from one of Ver-Age's homes. I think we got it. He's calming down. What you are seeing is this little guy. He must have been taken from his family when he was very young. In the beginning, a Ver-Age, this is what you are seeing, are calm and very friendly. They are smaller, but the effects of the gang have made them look frightening. This should wear off soon, since we caught most of his points. With this weather, he should be off to his family soon. Not to worry.

Whoa, DoC-tar, I believe we have more coming. Look over there. What is that?

Okay, this is not good everybody, run to the En-Circle. We're all in Carl, now we need your speed!

Doesn't look good, DoC there is boulders flying all over the place!

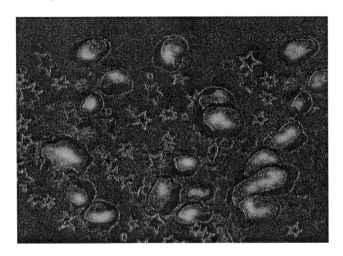

Yes, Carl this is one of our rock showers. Stay away from them if you can. I know this is dangerous, but we need to get to another trail as soon as possible.

Thanks, DoC, I just don't want to get turned around. SpellGet, what do you think of using some of the Bee Zee and Mr. Mores' dust? It might be able to help us here. I have to find that next trail.

Okay, duck your heads, everyone. This will be very bright. Okay, ready. *Just a Whoosh–Away* I think its working!

Everything is suspended. Go, Carl, go. Pen, have we seen a glimpse or glimmer yet?

Yes, we have, SpellGet, but there's another thing we've seen, and you're not going to like it. Watchem spotted the *Meteorocks* gang behind the rock shower. I guess they know we're here. Now what, DoC-tar?

Carl, we are near the Worthy galaxy, right?

Yes, just another left then right. But I must say, DoC-tar, now with them behind us, what can we do?

Pen, where did you see the glimpse?

It looks like it was glimmering from underneath the Random Acts stream. You were saying to GoTo and Newton that there are cracks in the stream, right?

You're right, Pen, but now I'm seeing the Whoosh-Away dust wearing off and right at the end of the rock shower. And yes, I believe they've spotted us, Carl, head for a trail nearest the stream. Newton, can you give Carl a hand.

I got it here, Carl. This one is the closest. It's right on the side. DoC, let us know what you want next.

Well, I hope no one is afraid of water. Because if we can hold these guys off long enough, we may have to jump in and find the crack where the glimmer is coming from. Okay everyone; grab your glove-'n'-paws and some of the berries. Remember, SpellGet, use that magic to get to all the berries so they will fly further, and maybe we can get lucky and slice off some of their sharp edges.

Okay, DoC-tar, but we still have the puffer shrooms. Wouldn't that be a better idea?

It would be, but we are too close to the Random Acts stream. Anything past this trail may spoil the stream. The best thing to do right now is to stir the *Meteorocks* so, hopefully, they will start to fight among themselves. Let's get started with the berries.

We will wait till we see it start, and then we can set down the puff shrooms right outside the *En-Circle*, and then we'll make a run for it. Hopefully, this will work. So are we all ready?

More than ready, DoC let's get these spear-carrying, family stealers, planet-demolishing thugs off our back!

Okay, everyone. On targets, fire! Just throw as many as you can. With the Bee-Zee dust, they should go just where you point them. Excellent, it looks like they are getting annoyed. They don't know where the blast is coming from. This is just what we wanted to see.

DoC-tar, I believe I am on the trail next to the Random Stream. What's next?

Okay, Carl, well done. We will be right back. SpellGet, Go-To, I think it's time to place the puffer

like me, except for DoC-tar Wishful and the big glowing furry guy. I know the DoC Well, this is interesting. May I ask why you are here?

Of course, I'll make this short—we are a team of searchers from StumpsVille. We are here trying to find a missing 'Past Key,' and there it was right here on your beach.

Well, it's not my beach, but I have been here for a long time. A 'Past Key' I have never seen one before. Is that what that thing is hmm . . . it has been throwing up blue lights through the cracks, I was never brave enough to go too close to it. Mrs. Sea told me just to stand back, and she was sure someone would be coming for it soon. That made me happy. I was really hoping it would be someone for me though.

Look at that SpellGet.

What is it Pen?

She's smiling. Good idea, DoC this may have made the whole search worthwhile, and of course, getting what we came for. Let's go over and introduce ourselves.

Well, hello, we were wondering if you could point us in the direction of Mrs. Sea's quarters. We need to speak with her. Sorry, I should have introduced myself first. I am Pen. This here is Watchem, Catchem, Newton, SpellGet, and Carl our Woofin, and you know DoC-tar Wishful, I believe.

Well, this is wonderful. Hello again, DoC-tar. It is nice to see you all. Mrs. Sea's quarters, yes, it's just down the shore here, that's where the large yellow structure on the slope is.

Okay, team, I will go and speak with her and find out if there is a backdoor to the Starcademy sphere. I haven't talk to her for a while, but I shouldn't be long. GoTo, you have a question?

Yes, DoC-tar, maybe ask if we might be able to bring A-Star with us, since she has been here for so long? Would you like that, A-Star? I'm getting a sense that you might.

Well, I believe I would love that. So where are you all from?

We are from StumpsVille in the Genuine galaxy. We are all called Stumpers, except for our Carl here. He's our very own special Woofin from another area of our land.

Okay, all of you, I'm on my way to see Mrs. Sea. Be back shortly.

Well, hello again, Mrs. Sea. It has been some time.

My old friend, DoC-tar Wishful, I thought that you would come for the shining blue lights. I haven't seen that in a long time. I knew it had to be one of your stars that owned it, am I correct? Is there something else I can help you with?

Yes, it is one of many of mine. It's a 'Past Key' and, yes, another favor. We were wondering if you may have a quicker trail to the Starcademy, maybe through the back. As you probably already know, the *Meteorocks* are swarming on the banks of the Random Acts stream.

Well, DoC-tar, you are right to the point here. I like that. Yes, we do have a trail, which I will show you here on the wall. There has been some spotting near that trail, but I'm sure you can either outrun them or have a method to divert them.

Yes, we do. One more thing, A-Star, may she join us to StumpsVille, where we believe she will fit right in? I am quite sure that was her beginnings before you found her on your shore.

I must say, DoC-tar, you have a lot to handle here. But about A-Star, I knew there would come the day she could be happy, but I must see her before you leave.

We will be leaving shortly. Sorry, but the time clock is ticking for this 'Past Key' to be replaced. Thank You, Mrs. Sea, for everything, and I will see you soon.

All right, DoC-tar Wishful, that is a date. You have always been a breath of fresh air. I will be by the trail to see you off and say my good-byes to A-Star and rest of you.

Okay, team, walk this way. A-Star, you're with us. SpellGet, start your *En-Circle*. Carl, we will need a lot of your paw power here. When you see the bright lights coming from the Starcademy, pull back. We should be able to slide right in under their sphere with the *En-Circle*, and you, being a Woofin recognized by the safe keepers, we won't have a problem.

We're all here, Carl, but Mrs. Sea would like to say her good-byes to A-Star before we leave. Okay, it's this trail and up we go. DoC-tar, I hate to bother you again, but look behind us. What should we do?

Sorry about that. We are just moving into another realm. Catchem, Watchem, can you hand out the glove-'n'-paws? We may need them again. It's interesting that the Riddlers knew we would have an extra passenger. Whatever comes toward us, just start throwing. GoTo, A-Star is here, please show her how to get up here on Carl.

Ok is everyone ready?

You bet, Carl!

Then hold on tight. We are on our way.

Watchem, what are you seeing? Is it one of them ray twister things that the DoC was talking about?

I'm sure it is Pen, and they look like their getting closer.

Okay, Stumpers, let's distract these guys. Go, Carl, go. Start throwing, and remember it doesn't matter about our aim, just see where you want it to blast.

Look at that. They are or going in the opposite direction, not toward us.

DoC-tar, I can see the light! Hold on, everybody, this is going to be a slide-in job, and it's on my left side, so keep right. There, we made it. Are you all okay?

Thanks, Carl, we're okay. Well done! Look over there, everyone. It's Mr. More on his step and our welcome-back branches, Maple, Oak, and Mayday.

Mr. More it is so nice to see you again. Thanks for waiting. We managed to get what we were searching for and met some interesting others along the way. Mayday, Oak, and Maple, so nice to see you too. Mayday could you refresh Carl on how to get down to the bottom again?

Of course that won't be a problem, Carl. Put your paws here and remember the leap to Oak, then it's down to Maple, and off to the field of Daze-zzys, where Page is. Nice to see you all of you again. I see you have another with you, and who might this be?

Hi, I'm A-Star. I was from the Sea of Seeing, but I have been offered to stay in StumpsVille with the help of these fine Stumpers.

Well, it is very nice to meet you. I'm sure we'll talk again. Till then, have a safe trip to the field of Daze-zzys.

Let's finish this, everyone. Carl, we're ready. Thanks again, Mr. More!

Okay, DoC-tar, I've got this. Down to Madam-a-la muse and then off to where *time slips away*, hold on everyone.

Great paw power Carl and we are just in time, Page is coming out of her dreams. Everyone please stand back. We have the key. Now, Page, I need you to turn on your side, and we will have this back in place in no time. There, good as new. Here, I will give you another burst of air, so you have some time to relax, okay?

DoC-tar Wishful, what happened? I can't remember anything. It was like I was dreaming.

Little one, don't worry. I will tell you all about it when we get home. Right now, I must go and thank the team that helped us. I will be back shortly. I know you're in good hands and paws here.

Well, Stumpers, it has been a pleasure working with all of you. You are a great search team. I will have to visit again, but not for the same reasons, I hope. You have become great friends of mine. Another thing, we should talk with Madam-a-la-Muse before Page and I have to leave, okay?

Sounds like a great idea, DoC You know the way, and we'll be right behind you. We all agree you must come and visit for any reason. You have been a friend to all of us too.

Madam! We are all here to explain the run-by.

No need to explain, little ones. I knew it had to be good news. Book Turner will be so happy to see Page back, and I know the ones that helped her will be honored. You all look tired, even Carl, but the best thing is you all came back. I am so proud of you. Now a great bit of advice, go home and get some rest. DoC-tar Wishful, you and yours, have a safe trip home. I know Page will be happy to see her family again.

Excuse me, Madam-a-la-Muse; maybe you can shine some light on this subject.

Yes, of course, Pen, you have a question?

Well, kind of, or maybe it's just a thought. I believe we have seen the sky for what it holds. Traveling through the different worlds has given all of us a better idea of how very similar we are. I know that there can be wonders beyond us and our imagination. There are great beings which are different yet the same in their kind ways. They definitely have their troubles too. In the end, I believe that we all agree that just a slight act of kindness can be just a wish away. This was not just a search but a journey. We all had our eyes wide opened. It wasn't that far from amazing.

You're right, Pen, and we all can learn from it. Thanks, Read-ER, for your great help. All of you have given yourselves a wonderful gift, ones of trust and friendship, like a great bond. Now with all that said, get your well-deserved rest. Till later, my friends, take care.

Okay, you heard the lady, now let's run. Last one to StumpsVille is a dirty puff shroom!

You said it, SpellGet, let's go, everyone!

Read-ER, I am so glad you were able to come with us. Thanks, and I hope we have the pleasure again. The truth from Madam was priceless. One more thing, give the present every moment it deserves, and always believe in yourself. Take care.

Oh . . . I'd better catch up to the team. There is no way I'm going to be the dirty puff shroom *today*.

Well, look at you, Carl waiting for me. That's great, you big glowing beauty. Let's catch up.

Well, I just thought I'd give them a head start, SpellGet.

Woof!

About the Author, Illustrator

Bev Scholz
Lives in northern Alberta, Canada
With the muse of Muses and dogs of Dawgs.
Loves all things creative.
A published illustrator of
books and short stories,
a recognized photographer (a passion)
And an Author with more than a few stories
But
Believes in just a few things
To live, love and laugh in our everyday journey.
To live this day to the fullest
To Love is to say I love you more,
Laugh, from your insides out
Just Believe.
BZ

CPSIA information can be obtained
at www.ICGtesting.com
Printed in the USA
LVOW11s0016050817
543766LV00001B/45/P

9 781490 779973